T0369277

BUTTERFLY!

Order this book online at www.trafford.com
or email orders@trafford.com

For information or to purchase book(s) check your local bookstore; or, contact author at
809 E. Bloomingdale Ave ~~ Box #240, Brandon, FL 33511.

Most Trafford titles are also available at major online book retailers.

Tom Michel, Editor
My Son, Robin, Advisor
Critiqued by my sister Ramona, my Daughter-in-law Janis, and by a neighbor Cheryl Rickert
Cover Design by Lois Barnes
Author Cover Art and all other illustrations, copyright free

Quotations from "The Gnostic Bible", edited by Willis Barnstone and Marvin Meyer,
© 2003 by Willis Barnstone and Marvin Meyer. Reprinted by arrangement with Shambhala
Publications, Inc., www.shambhala.com.

Quotations from "The Dead Sea Scrolls Bible: The Oldest Known Bible Translated for the
First Time into English, © 1999 by Martin Abegg, Jr., Peter Flint, and Eugene Ulrich.
HarperCollins Publishers, http://www.harpercollins.com

Printed in Victoria, BC, Canada.

ISBN: 978-1-4251-6227-6 (soft)
ISBN: 978-1-4251-6228-3 (ebook)

www.trafford.com

North America & international
toll-free: 1 888 232 4444 (USA & Canada)
phone: 812 355 4082

*"Dreams are not so different from deeds
as some may think.
All the deeds of men are only dreams
at first.
And in the end, their deeds dissolve
into dreams."*

Theodore Herzl, Old New Land, 1902

*"All that is valuable in human society
depends upon the opportunity
for development
accorded the individual."*

Albert Einstein

DEDICATED TO

My Spiritual Guide
["Thank You" for "Odd Ball" and
For "Coda"]

My son, Robin
My daughter-in-law, Janis
My granddaughters:
Bailey and Madison

My brother, Norman
My sisters:
Ramona, Nancy, and Rita
My sister-in-law Marie
My brothers-in-law
Elmore, Joe, and Donnie

Also to

Tom, Joan, Thomas, Chuck, Mark,
David, Claudia, and Julie

And

In Loving Memory of

My parents
Elizabeth M. and James E. Prewitt

My Sisters
Mary Elizabeth and Norma Jean

"We were two
and had but one heart between us."

Francois Villon

"Your vision will become clear
only when you look into your heart . . . .
Who looks outside, dreams,
who looks inside, awakens."

Carl Jung

"The real price of every thing,
what every thing really costs
to the man who wants to acquire it,
is the toil and trouble of acquiring it."

Adam Smith, The Wealth of Nations, 1776

CONTENTS

"You see things and you say 'Why?',
but I dream things that never were
and I say, 'Why not?'"

George Bernard Shaw

FOREWORD

Many commentators as well as authors of dictionaries, usage guides, editors, teachers, and others feel strongly that such "absolute" words as *complete, equal, perfect,* and especially ***UNIQUE*** cannot be compared because of their "meaning". The statement that a thing is either ***Unique*** or it is not, has often been repeated. Objections are based chiefly on the assumption that ***Unique*** has but a single absolute sense, an assumption contradicted by information readily available in dictionaries.

In modern use both comparison and modification are widespread and standard. When either sense is intended, ***Unique*** is used without qualifying modifiers. Comparison of so-called absolutes in senses that are not absolute is standard in all varieties of speech and writing.

It is also my belief that avid and serious readers always keep a dictionary close at hand for the occasional new word, or words they want to learn or to clarify. Hence, on page 61 begins a quick reference dictionary of selected words for the readers' convenience, interest, and amusement.

Fantastically speaking, this story is ***Unique***, should it be a dream, day-dream, muse, fantasy, or, factual! Whether you view Butterfly as dream, fantasy, metaphysical, astrological, religious, or factual, I trust you to enjoy it for its own merits, and, I thank you for your interest!—*Lois Barnes*

*"A soft answer
turneth away wrath,
but grievous words
stir up anger."*

Proverbs 15:1

"Everyone thinks of changing the world,
but no one thinks
of changing himself"

Leo Tolstoi

BUTTERFLY!

By Lois B. Barnes

"No one is truly literate who cannot read his own heart."

Eric Hoffer

It was midday and Elouise was strolling around looking out the second floor windows and down upon the street.

1

Suddenly she cried out: "Oh, look at that poor old man and that young boy! I feel sorry for them because they are so strange!"

Keith and I ran to the windows to see what was the matter!

Sure enough there was an old, old, man trudging *eastward* along the side of the street. Following closely, in stride, as if in his very tracks, was a very young boy.

The old man was tall and very thin. So was the young boy. The old man was

2

leaning so far back that his nose and his Adam's apple were pointed straight up to the sun-filled sky!

The young boy was leaned back in the very same way! My, they did indeed look strange! In fact, they were so incredibly thin they looked just like stick people!

I stood watching them move jerkily along. Their every move was synchronous!

Each lifted his right leg up with a jerk, placed his right foot to the ground with a jerk, lifted his left leg up with a jerk, placed his left foot to the ground with a jerk.

The two were not connected—yet they moved as if they were . . . . .

As if they were . . . . . Robots!

Yes, they seemed very strange, **very strange indeed!**

But, unlike Elouise, I did not feel sorry for them, because, I was fast becoming aware of something.

When friends or others look sad,
    or even bad,
Or maybe strange, or disarranged,
Usually it is a blatant, though silent, plea
For <u>someone to understand</u>, or,
    <u>for someone to see,</u>
They really are much better
Then they now appear to be!

I became very excited because something inside me was sensing that indeed they were different, and far better, than what they now appeared to be.

Then, unexpectedly, and without prior *conscious* thought, I heard myself excitedly declare to Keith and Elouise:

"There is only one! Because of the way they look, you think there are two! But, there is really only one!"

Wide-eyed and gaping mouths, they both looked at me with disdain, skepticism, and disbelief!

I even surprised myself when un-abashed, unfettered, and unrestrained, I began yelling ever so loudly!

"Look, look, there is only one! There is only one! There is only one!"

I shouted so loud that the old man and the young boy, hearing, yet never missing a step, nor slackening their pace, *simultaneously* turned their faces around, and looked up at me!

I *knew* then for certain

That what seemed to be

An old man and a young boy

Were not at all

As they appeared to be!

Something inside me

Was telling me so!

7

You can imagine how excited I became then! Thrilled by the energized atmosphere of probability, I now bellowed as loudly as I possibly could!

"There is only one! There is only one! **Look!! Look!! There is only one!!**" Something inside me was so sure!

Just then, a bright flash

Of silver-white light

Exploded all around them!!

At once they were changed

Into child-size twins

And, they were holding

Each other's hands!

Now that was quite startling, and most unusual for something to change that way!

Keith and Elouise were frightened! So was I!

But, something deep inside me just **_knew_** it was going to be all right.

I was in the lead, as we ran as fast as we could down the stairs and out onto the

9

street. My thought was to help them, if only I could!

And, of course, I kept yelling, "There is only one! There is only one! There is *absolutely* only one!"

Well! The changes were not over! And our excitement intensified—because, through a sudden wafting blur, *WE SAW THE TWO BECOME ONE!!!*

That ONE was now a cute, fat, cat-size creature with several legs and two humps upon its back!

It darted spasmodically about with quite amazing speed!

It ran toward me and scampered and climbed around, running over my feet and legs!

Elouise screamed and jumped backward! Keith ran to the other side of the street!

It continued to move over and around my feet and legs. Soon it sensed that I was not afraid, and I *knew* it was not afraid of me.

It came to rest stretched against the outside calf of my left leg. It had changed again, was extremely small, had no legs, and only one hump upon its back.

Never, never, in all my life have I ever, ever, wanted any creepy, crawly, slimy, things to crawl on me, even if they were cute!

One time, very long ago, before my folks could get a tiny wood tick off me, you would have thought, by the way I behaved, that I was a wild and screaming **banshee**! I was so scared!

12

But, this time something inside me decided not to be afraid.

I knew what I was observing was the very same life force as before!

Once again, its aspect only **moved, acted, and looked, different**.

Somehow, now for sure, *I knew* it only needed something, or someone, to re-mind it to believe in itself!

I reached down and *peeled* "IT" off my leg.

I gently held it cupped in both my hands.

Then I spoke out loud—I strongly, *fervently* affirmed to it:

"No! You cannot park yourself here! And I am not going to let you crawl around on your belly, nor to become a leach!"

At that precise moment, the most astounding, profound, remarkable thing occurred!

I saw not larva, nor Chrysalis! Only a spark of silver light; then, red brilliance! And—Snap! Crack! Swish!

A metamorphic *incident*—in a fragment of time!

<u>Instantly</u>, it had turned into the biggest, the most beautiful, translucent, bright red butterfly one could ever hope to see!

It was so huge it filled both my hands! My mouth fell open! I was speechless! I was amazed! I was stunned!

My head was in a whirl from all the

concentrated attention ~ ~ ~ ! !

But something deep within my heart

was exceedingly happy! It was stupendous!

It was mysterious! It was exciting!

I could feel the **healthy life** in its

shiny jet-black body pulsating against my

fingers!

The sunlight shimmered and glis-

tened on its extraordinary, brilliant, irides-

cent wings!

The gentle breeze fluttered its delicate ruffled wingtips!

This spectacular butterfly resembled the wide gleaming arched petals of a flower called Iridaceae—Iris; nicknamed Flag!

Immediately the spectacular red butterfly started to fly away! But quickly, I caught it!

I wanted to keep it!

I wanted to have it for my own!

I wanted to take it home with me!

I wanted to care for it in my room!

But . . . . something inside me *knew* that would not be best.

"Well," I thought excitedly, "I'll get a big outdoor cage to keep it in for every- one to see."

But, again, something inside me would not accept that idea either.

I stood there, holding "MY" special, spectacular, red butterfly.

I so wanted it to be mine!

18

But, I *knew*, I must fully consider what I really should do.

Then . . . . . it did something that you may think peculiar, and really question or wonder about!

It pooped—dribbling down both my arms!

Oh, yes it did!

It did!

It did!

Astonished, I took two or three steps backward; yet, maintained my hold upon the beautiful, red butterfly.

I must have looked bewildered, per-plexed, surprised, as <u>immediately</u>, a man came briskly along!

Abruptly, and in a ***<u>daring</u>*** and deep, gruff, smugly authoritative voice, he said:

"The only reason it is doing that, is because it is afraid!"

Like the extreme searing force of a lightning strike came my anger!!!

Clearly it was his intent to *intimidate* me by flagrantly emanating his presumed, self-assumed, authority!

Barely maintaining control, I quickly turned, determined to ignore him, and just walk away!

Instead, I stopped in my tracks—and seriously thought about it—cocking my head from side to side, as one sometimes does when engaged in inner conversation.

I took my time——

Then——very slowly——albeit intentionally——I turned back around and forthrightly confronted him!

"No! Sir! It is not afraid!," I firmly stated.

"I can feel its body and its quiet pulsating life! I **_know_** it trusts me!

22

"And, in its own way, it has plainly expressed something so very, very, much more important **than apparently YOU are able to perceive!**"

"Well then," not convinced and with an obtrusive, swaggering, bemused, although obtuse conduct, and even greater sternness, he aggressively harangued at me:

"It is doing that because it is not yet very old . . . yap, yap, yap . . . yap, yap . . yap, yap, yap . . . . ." he just blubbered, prattled, blathered, and chattered . . . . on and on and on . . . . Whoa! This bigot made me wonder about his thought processes.

Quite obviously, he had become confounded, disturbed, and exceedingly agitated because I would not blindly, submissively, obediently, and compliantly agree with **his** self-proclaimed, man-ordained, pre-supposed, so-called 'male superiority!'

He, *inappropriately*, thought he knew all the answers you see!

Even though it had just become a beautiful, spectacular, brilliant, red butterfly, in my heart I **_knew_** that the life force it expressed <u>had nothing to do with age</u>, and quite frankly, **I told him so!**

"The *conscious* awareness of that which truly defines the butterfly, or me, or <u>even you</u>, Sir . . . . .

"Most assuredly, <u>comes only from deep within one's self</u>, from an inner con-tact to one's higher consciousness!

<u>"ONE'S SPIRIT</u>

<u>COMES FROM</u>

<u>ONE'S SOURCE OF BEING!</u>

"Definitely, Sir, one's highest conscious awareness does not come from anyone else, nor from any other's concepts, or any social whims, or popular widespread religious beliefs!

"Nor does one's Spirit come from science, lawyers, politicians, from any government, or the world at large!

"ONE'S SPIRIT DOES NOT

COME FROM

ANYONE,

OR ANYTHING ELSE!

"Each one's direct contact to our Source is available and readily facilitated precisely through each one's own inner, heartfelt, bedrock of <u>direct knowing</u>, _'the still small voice'_!"

All the while, Keith had been watching everything from across the street. He ran over to us and diplomatically announced:

"I heard about a book you can buy that will tell you all about what just happened."

I deliberately looked at Keith, long

and slow ~~~~~~~~

Thinking and contemplating all the

while ~~~~~~~~

Because he was a very good friend,

with whom I had walked many a mile!

I also knew Keith was exceedingly

bright, **and cautioning me that things**

don't always go the way we would like!

Additionally, this was his attempt to quell a possible fight!!

Confidently, I smiled at him and said: "Thank you, Keith. But, I need not consult another book.

"Because, I already know the answer myself!"

My every decisive heartbeat was telling me so!

I most surely *knew* that "MY" beau-

tiful red butterfly was straightforward, un-

flinching, and totally sincere, in giving me

its message, the only way it could!!!

It was the effervescence——No . . . . .

More a vivacious aliveness

In the intelligence it conveyed

By pooping on me!

An offensive act—

In deliberate defiance!

Of being held—

Against its will—

In captivity!

Those who were present just did not comprehend its exceptional signal!

Of course, that was all right too.

But I am sure you understand

All about things like this,

Don't you?

And, you probably already know what I did with "MY" beautiful, spectacular, exceptional, red butterfly.

31

Yes, I absolutely *knew* what I actually must do!

So I stretched out my arms and held it up high, and, **<u>THAT</u>** special, beautiful, unique, spectacular, incredible, red butterfly, flew directly over to the full-bloom cherry tree!

It flitted and fluttered from bloom to bloom, as one often sees bright yellow butterflies consistently do, around the yellow-flowered butterfly trees!

Surprisingly, it came straight back to me! Circling, it landed on my arm, then, on my shoulder; on my head; on my face!

__I KNEW__ this was it's way of saying "GOODBYE" to me!

And, __just like that__—it gracefully went upward and onward into the clear blue sky!

Free, free—with rightful equivalency! For it had finally, __definitely__ become what it was intended to be!

As I stood watching its stunning, vivid, colorful ascent, its grateful acknowledgment rained down upon me!

An intense, stupendous, amazing, dazzling array!

Iridescent reds, blues, greens, platinum, silver, and gold!

Flowing, twinkling, sparkling, *minute'* particles—symbols! Symbols all. Symbols—of Love, of Truth, of Wisdom, of Knowledge.

Now, of course, everyone can see—

Truly, it is *Unique! <u>UNIQUE</u>!*

{When an unusual personal situation or occurrence takes place in one's life that leaves one profoundly changed, enlightened, informed, and/or advanced, *<u>that particular encounter should definitely be considered UNIQUE to that person, animal, bird, or, butterfly!</u>*}

And it is definitely <u>Far</u>, <u>Far</u>, <u>FAR</u> greater than it originally appeared to be!

All it had really needed

Was sincere

Consistent

Encouragement!

From someone—like you!

Or, someone—like me!!

A very special someone!

A dependable, forthright,

AUTHENTIC FRIEND!

Although this time,

Explicitly,

Unequivocally,

Absolutely!

It had to come

From the only one

Who could assist it

In its completion!

This Time——-

That Friend——

That One—

THAT

RESPONSIBLE

ONE

OF COURSE,

COULD ONLY BE

ME!!

The End

CODA

It has been said, and even in the absence of conclusive proof I agree, that the <u>right side of our brain</u> is essentially endowed with the natural creative capacity, power, and ability of ***intuition, inner spatial abilities,*** and ***nonverbal thinking,*** which are primarily attributed to **females.**

It has been said, and again in the absence of conclusive proof I agree, that the <u>left side of our brain</u> is essentially endowed with the natural creative capacity, power, and ability of ***logic, reason,*** and ***mathematical abilities,*** which are primarily attributed to **males.**

41

Factually, when not hampered, maligned, nor interfered with, our minds work very well with these naturally creative thinking attributes regardless of the sexual orientation of the body into which we are born. Additionally, it does not matter in what part of the world we happen to be born!

Each one's psychological, physical, mental, and spiritual growth and development as well as one's trials and errors and various other changes are accomplished at their own individual speeds for very profound reasons! In order to reach one's highest, one must be willing to take risks or chances—but, with caution!

Astrologically speaking, astrology is a study of the stars and their strong or subtle, but direct effects or influences on ourselves, on our world, and on all life. Certainly everyone should understand the effects and the necessity of the sun and the moon, <u>because they are so obvious</u>! Not so obvious are the effects of the other planets and stars upon our lives! Not only astronomically, but also astrologically!

You could spend a lot of time studying and gaining insight and knowledge of yourself, and others, from astrology without ever getting involved with horoscopes. And, of course, you need not study astronomy, astrology, or anything, in order to live your life.

However, the point I am making is that **unless, or until,** YOU PERSONALLY take the time to study for the knowledge and enlightenment that can be attained from astrology, *or, for that matter, from any past, present, or future field of study,* **how can you *"in strict honesty"* make an informed decision, or a fair and balanced judgment about them—for anyone, but specifically for yourself?**

While the "authorities" disagree, as they do about most things, but especially about astrology, <u>anything less than your own</u> in-depth, sincere, and honest investigative study is conflicted, tainted, or erroneous judgment!

Judgment, whether acceptance, nonacceptance, sympathy, empathy, or ridicule, when it is based on a lack of personally obtained knowledge, or, when based upon *someone else's beliefs,* **is ignorance! Abso-**

lute ignorance!

Not only does this lack of knowledge and discernment set precedent for a lazy, scoffing habit of harmful ridicule and put-downs, but ignorance can make us subject to devious, lie-laden rule by dictators, or worse!

Religiously speaking, there are more *"sacred beliefs"* than can be imagined! In fact, the word "belief" itself is an interesting study. But, for those who rely on **any** *specific religious history*, **be advised, there is MUCH you are NOT being told!** Deliberately so, I hasten to add!

For example, regarding the guidance of stars, there is this little recognized and not so well known, **Directive of The Lord**

45

from the Dead Sea Scrolls, Cave Four, Jar Number Four: *"The Lord has spoken, 'do not allow your discouragement to overcome you, but rather rejoice in the truth that I have indeed sent help to you from The Stars'."*

Although not about stars, another not so well known and rarely acknowledged religious/historical example which seems to be giving a lot of people a mental trial, is from **the Gnostic Bible Wisdom Gospel Of Thomas, Part 1 Hidden Saying #22:** **[1]Jesus upon seeing infants being suckled tells his disciples, [2]"these nursing babies are like those who enter the kingdom."** The disciples asked, **"Then, shall we enter the kingdom as babies?"**

[1]Most infants were not suckled beyond age two during that time.
[2]At that time there were those who generally believed that all infants were pure in thought until around age two.

Jesus replied: **"When you make the two into one, and when you make the inner as the outer, and the upper into the lower, and when you make male and female into a single one, so that the male shall not be male, and the female shall not be female, then, you will enter the kingdom."**

Yes, it is understandable why this is such a challenge!

Now, permit me my interpretation, which follows in italics:

Jesus replied: "When you make the two *[the masculine energies and the feminine energies]* into one, and when you make the inner as the outer, *[expressing outwardly what Spirit reveals from within]*

47

and the upper into the lower, *[integrate balanced thought processes with a cooperative ego]* and when you make male and female *[masculine and feminine thinking attributes]* into a single one, so that the male shall not be male, *[stuck in only thinking with the masculine left brain in charge]* and the female shall not be female, *[stuck in only thinking with the feminine right brain in charge]* then, *[and only then]* you will enter the kingdom. *[Into direct knowing—like little children whose thinking remains pure and has not yet been contaminated by those who teach and train them in the particular society into which they happen to be born!]*

These are among the most sensible little known and rarely acknowledged "historical/religious" records I have yet come across—and conceivably support my maintained proposition of what "humankind" should and could become— each one of us, from within—*our own ego, our two-part brain, and our Spirit*— become united as **_one_** in direct connection to our ***"_still small voice_" where direct knowing——direct contact with our source——is facilitated!***

Dream wise there are many kinds of dreams and many reasons or causes for dreams. In the Contract I have with my Publisher there is one question that I have found to be a definite challenge:

Subject matter
Please indicate the appropriate subject for your book. Choose from these categories:

- Fiction
- Children's Fiction
- Non Fiction
- Children's Non Fiction

First, this book is for all ages and both sexes. Further, in my opinion, dreams are real in the sense that you really dream—the energies actually flow! Sleep time dreams can be shallow, profound, prophetic, or even messages from God—and when so, are always symbolic!

Dreams—especially prophetic and/or profound ones—are real as opposed to fiction! Whether or not a person understands or can discern, perceive, or fathom their own dreams may be questionable. In the final analysis however, the dreamer is the only one who can really know!

Some people claim they never

dream. Could be true, but I doubt that. More than likely they just do not remember. Although, when you consider the variability of people worldwide, humans do range from near perfection to aberration—psychologically, physically, and/or mentally—quite conceivably there is someone who never dreams.

Some people even have nightmares or phantasmagorias that really do frighten them.

I have had many repetitive dreams—one reoccurring during pregnancy until I was able to remember every detail of it. It proved itself to me to be prophetic and profound! This book is about another prophetic, profound, and real dream I continue to experience the meaning of! So, yes, of my publisher's four choices, *I know* this book is ***non-fiction*** and ***symbolically real!***

Actually, it is **o**ur own recognition, acknowledgement, and the balanced use of our own two-part dual-function brain, **in cooperation** with our body, and our Spirit, *that is necessary* for each of us to be one complete balanced person! ***This inner balance is required in order to respond with "equanimity" in our outer behavior, and in our acceptance, and treatment of self and others!*** Hence, we should not be separate disconnects; rather, we could be one— bodily, mentally, and spiritually united— within! ***There should only be one!***

From life's experiences I had already learned that what we are constantly taught, the ideas with which we are consistently ingrained, what our expected behavior leads us to become, **IS directly responsible for how we compare ourselves to others, where we see ourselves "placed" in our own "group(s)", as well as to the definite effects of the "centuries old" erroneous beliefs about our minds and our bodies!**

Not only that, but every culture believes itself to be "the best" and always on "the right—the correct—the appropriate—the approved" side of God! Our American culture happens to be quite arrogant in the belief that we are the best people existing—in the entire world!

Those age old beliefs have caused

us to concentrate too much on our possessions, on our physical body, on our body behavior, on what we believe is our just due, on what our money can obtain. Also, on how much of the world we can command or control, and flauntingly on where our money can place us—all at the expense of our irreplaceable thinking attributes and on our abilities to get along!

This has already proven to result in critical and damaging imbalances that can be seen in people all over the world!

For example, males who do not recognize the feminine thinking attributes, abilities, and capabilities *within themselves,* **always fail** to recognize Women as equals! Too many males around the world have **to-**

tally failed in this regard **and ignorantly and arrogantly** consider themselves superior to all females!

This horrendous world-wide fallacy by males has resulted in and manifests as unspeakable abuses of women and female children! **Actually, these callous males are radically imbalanced—warped in and by their own indoctrinated thinking!**

Women who do not recognize the masculine thinking attributes, abilities, and capabilities within themselves also fail to live up to their own potentials and may feel inferior!

When a person, an individual, has been subjected, indoctrinated, and/or brain-washed, within their particular culture, **[especially when he or she is consciously aware of their own personally differing views, but having already been silenced, restricted, and/or immobilized]**, they can and usually do, become imbalanced, er-ratic, take on inconsistent actions, behav-iors, and/or appearances, and are treated accordingly by **their ignorant and arro-gant peers**!

Everyone undergoes challenges and

a variety of situations throughout their individual lives! But, it is all about physical, mental, and psychological growth, development, learning, unfoldment, and expression.

The difference between being considered balanced or imbalanced, is, perhaps, in how, and whether or not <u>one</u> has acquiesced, accepted, and willingly or forcefully fit into their particular culture or society!

<u>And it depends</u> on how well each <u>one actually is</u> accepted, or rejected, by that same society! But the <u>main distinction de-</u>

pends upon whether or not each one stands by their own inner convictions, proofs, certainties, and knowings——-irregardless of what others may think, say, or do!

Finally, and most certainly, a healthy body requires a good healthy blood supply. Blood is the circulation of our life, our life support, life enduring, life itself—the vital principle. Life! Blood is the fluid that circulates in the heart, arteries, capillaries, and veins carrying nourishment and oxygen to and bringing away waste products from all parts of the body. Blood is **_Red_** and represents health! This *Butterfly* is red!

"What did you learn today?
Did you learn what to believe,
or,
did you learn how to think?"

Ralph Nader
The Seventeen Traditions, 2007

"Character is not inherited!
We build it daily by the way we
Individually think and act,
Thought by thought,
Action by action!
When you let fear, hate, or anger
Take possession of your mind,
They become self-forged chains!"

Unknown

Cowardice asks, Is it safe?
Expediency asks, Is it polite?
Vanity asks, Is it popular?
But Conscience asks,
Is it right?

Pushon

Convenient
Quick Reference
Selected Words
Dictionary
For The Young At Heart

- **Ab-er-ra-tion** *n.* The act of departing from the right, normal, or usual course; the act of deviating from the ordinary, usual, or normal type; deviation from truth or moral rectitude; mental irregularity or disorder, especially of a minor or temporary nature; lapse from a sound mental state. Wandering; deviation, divergence, abnormality, eccentricity, illusion, delusion, hallucination.

- **Ab-so-lute-ly** *adv.* Without exception; completely; wholly; entirely: *You are absolutely right.* Positively; certainly. Used emphatically to express complete agreement or unqualified assent: *Do you think it will work? Absolutely!* Totally, unqualifiedly, unquestionably, unequivocally, definitely.

- **Ag-i-tate** *v.* To move or force into violent, irregular action: *The hurricane winds agitated the sea.* To shake or move briskly. To move to and fro; impart regular motion to. To disturb or excite emotionally; arouse; perturb: *a crowd agitated to a frenzy by impassioned oratory.* To call attention to by speech or writing; discuss; debate. To consider all sides; revolve in the mind; plan; arouse; attempt to arouse public interest and support, as in some political or social cause or theory. Disturb, toss, wave, ruffle, fluster, roil, dispute. **Ag-i-tat-ed,** *adj.* **Ag-i-ta-tor** *n.*

- **Al-be-it** *conj.* Although; even if: *a peaceful, albeit brief retirement.*

- **A-live** *adj.* Having life; living; existing; not dead or lifeless. Living (used for emphasis): *the proudest man alive.* In a state of action; in force or operation; active: *to keep hope alive.* Full of energy and spirit; lively: *Grandmother's more alive than most of her contemporaries.* Having the quality of life; vivid; vibrant: *The room was alive with color.* **Alive to,** alert or sensitive to; aware of: *City planners are alive to the necessity of revitalizing deteriorating neighborhoods.* **Alive with,** filled with living things; swarming; teeming: *The room was alive with mosquitoes.* **Look alive!** Pay attention! Move quickly! *Look alive! We haven't got all day.* Active. **A-liveness,** *n.*

- **Ar-ro-gant** *adj.* Making claims or pretensions to superior importance or rights; overbearingly assuming; insolently proud: *an arrogant public official.* Characterized by or proceeding from arrogance: *arrogant claims,* presuming, presumptuous, haughty, imperious, brazen. **Ar-ro-gant-ly,** *adv.* <u>*AND* **from Ambrose Bierce's profound book, "The Devil's Dictionary"**</u>: **Arrogant** as in **Aristocracy** n.: Government by the best men. (In this sense the word is obsolete; so is that kind of government.) Fellows that wear downy hats and clean shirts—guilty of education and suspected of bank accounts!

- **As-sured** *adj.* To declare earnestly to; inform or tell positively; state with confidence to: *She assured us that everything would turn out all right.* To cause to know surely; reassure. To pledge or promise; give surety of; guarantee: *He was assured a job in the spring.* To make (a future event) sure; ensure. To secure or confirm; render safe or stable. To give confidence to; encourage. Guaranteed; sure; certain; secure. Bold; confident; authoritative. Boldly presumptuous. **As-sur-ed-ly,** *adv.*

- **As-ton-ish** *v.t.* To fill with sudden and overpowering surprise or wonder; amaze: *Her easy humor and keen intellect astonished me.* astound, startle, shock. See **surprise.**

- **Au-then-tic** *adj.* Not false or copied; genu-

63

ine; real. Having the origin supported by un-questionable evidence; authenticated; veri-fied: *an authentic document of the Middle Ages.* Entitled to acceptance or belief because of agreement with known facts or experience; reliable; trustworthy. Original, primary, first hand, one who does things himself. AUTHEN-TIC, GENUINE, REAL, VERITABLE share the sense of actuality and lack of falsehood or misrep-resentation. AUTHENTIC carries a connotation of authoritative certification that an object is what it is claimed to be.

- **Bal-ance** *n., v.* Being harmonious, in proper arrangement or adjustment, proportion, etc.; fair, equitable, just, impartial, evenhanded; a state of equilibrium or equipoise; equal distri-bution of weight, amount, etc.; something used to produce equilibrium; counterpoise; mental steadiness or emotional stability; habit of calm behavior, judgment, etc.; a state of bodily equilibrium.

- **Ban-shee** *n.* In Irish folklore, as well as in Gaelic folklore, a Banshee is a spirit in the form of a wailing woman who appears to or is heard by members of a family as a sign that one of them is about to die, or, that someone in that house will soon die. Also, woman of a fairy mound.

- **Be-ing** *n.* The fact of existing; existence (as opposed to nonexistence). Conscious, mortal existence; life: *Our being is as an instantaneous flash of light in the midst of eternal night.* Substance or nature: *of such a being as to arouse fear.* Something that exists. A living thing. A human being; person: *the most beautiful being you could imagine.* God. That which has actuality either materially or in idea. Absolute existence in a complete or perfect state, lacking no essential characteristic; essence. *Nonstandard.*

• **Bi-got** *n.* A person who is utterly intolerant of any differing creed, belief, or opinion; a derogatory name. **_AND_ from The D's Dictionary:** One who is obstinately and zealously attached to an opinion that you do not entertain.

• **Blath-er** *n.* Foolish, voluble talk. To talk or utter foolishly; blither; babble: *The poor thing blathered for hours about the intricacies of his psyche.* Blether, to chatter, blabber.

• **Blith-er** *v.i.* To talk foolishly; blather: *He's blithering about some problem of his.*

• **Blur** *v.* To obscure or sully (something) by smearing or with a smeary substance: *The windows were blurred with soot,* to obscure by making confused in form or outline; make indistinct: *The fog blurred the outline of the car,* to dim the perception or susceptibility of; make dull or insensible: *The blow on the* *head blurred his senses;* to become indistinct: *Everything blurred as she ran.* To make blurs, a smudge or smear that obscures. A blurred condition; indistinctness. To cloud, dim, darken, veil, mask. B-l-u-r-r-r . . . .

- **Brain** n. *__From__ __The D's Dictionary__:* An apparatus with which we think that we think. That which distinguishes the man who is content to *be* something from the man who wishes to *do* something. A man of great wealth, or one who has been pitch-forked into high station, has commonly such a head-full of brain that his neighbors cannot keep their hats on. In our civilization, and under our demo-repub repub-licrat *form of government,* brain is so highly honored that it is rewarded by exemption from the cares of office!

- **Brain-wash** *v.t.* To cause (someone) to undergo brainwashing. The process of brainwashing; a subjection to brainwashing; a method for systematically changing attitudes or altering beliefs! Originated in totalitarian countries, especially through the use of torture, drugs, or psychological-stress techniques. Any method of controlled systematic indoctrination; especially one based on repetition and/or confusion: *brainwashing by TV commercials.* An instance of subjecting or being subjected to such techniques.

- **Brisk** *adj.* Quick and active; lively: *brisk*

trading; a brisk walk. Sharp and stimulating; abrupt; curt: *I was surprised by her rather brisk tone.* To make or become brisk; liven (often followed by *up*). Spry, energetic, alert. **Brisk-ly**, *adv.*

- **Cage** *n.* A boxlike enclosure having wires, bars, or the like, for confining and displaying birds or animals. Anything that confines or imprisons; prison. Something resembling a cage in structure. Any skeleton framework, steel framework, or retainer. To put or confine in or as if in a cage. Birdcage, pen, coop, enclosure, pound.

- **Calf** *n.,* The fleshy part of the back of the human leg below the knee.

- **Cal-lous** *adj.* Made hard; hardened, insensitive; indifferent; unsympathetic: *They have a callous attitude toward the sufferings of others.* Having a callous; indurated, as parts of the skin exposed to friction. To make or become hard or callous. Hard-skinned, tough skin, any hard substance; inured, insensible, obtuse. See hard. *AND* **from The D's Dictionary:** Gifted with great fortitude to bear the evils afflicting another!

- **Cap-i-tal** n. The city or town that is the official seat of government in a country, state, etc. A city regarded as being of special eminence in some field of activity: *New York is* *the dance capital of the world..* The wealth, whether in money or property, owned or employed in business by an individual, firm, corporation, etc.; an accumulated stock of such wealth. Any form of wealth employed or capable of being employed in the production of more wealth. Any source of profit, advantage, power, etc.; asset. Capitalists as a group or class (distinguished from *labor*): Pertaining to financial capital. Principal; highly important. Chief, especially as being the official seat of government of a country, state, etc. Excellent or first-rate: *a capital hotel.* Involving the loss of life: *capital punishment*—punishable by death: *a capital offender.* Fatal; extremely serious. Principal, investment, assets, stock. Prime, primary, first. The adjectives CAPITAL, CHIEF, MAJOR, PRINCIPAL apply to a main or leading representative of a kind. CAPITAL may mean larger or more prominent; it may also suggest preeminence or excellence: *capital letter, idea, virtue,* etc. ***AND* from The D's Dictionary:** The seat of misgovernment. That which provides the fire, the pot, the dinner, the table, and the knife and fork for the anarchist; the part of the repast that himself supplies is the disgrace before meat. *Capital Punishment,* a penalty regarding the justice and expediency of which many worthy persons—including all the assassins—entertain grave misgivings!

• **Cap-tiv-i-ty** *n.* The state or period of being

held, imprisoned, enslaved, or confined. Bondage, servitude, slavery, thralldom, subjection; imprisonment, confinement, incarceration.

- **Cau-tion** *n.* Alertness and prudence in a hazardous situation; care; wariness: *Landslides ahead—proceed with caution.* A warning against danger or evil; anything serving as a warning: *By way of caution, he told me the difficulties I would face. Informal.* a person or thing that astonishes or causes mild apprehension: *She's a caution. The way he challenges your remarks is a caution.* To give warning to; advise or urge to take heed. To warn or advise: *The newspapers caution against overoptimism.* Circumspection, discretion, watchfulness, heed, vigilance, admonition, advice, counsel, admonish, forewarn. See warn.

- **Chat-ter** *v.i.* To talk rapidly in a foolish or purposeless way; jabber. To utter a succession of quick, inarticulate, speechlike sounds, as monkeys or certain birds. To make a rapid clicking noise by striking together: *His teeth were chattering from the cold..* To utter rapidly or purposelessly. To cause to chatter, as the teeth from cold. Purposeless or foolish talk. The act or sound of chattering.

- **Chrys-a-lis** *n.* The hard-shelled pupa of a moth or butterfly; an obtect pupa.

- **Co-da** *n.* A more or less independent passage, at the end of a composition, introduced to bring it to a satisfactory close. A concluding section or part, especially one of a conventional form and serving as a summation of preceding themes, motifs, etc., as in a work of literature or drama. Anything that serves as a concluding part.

- **Com-plete** *adj.* Having all parts or elements; lacking nothing; whole; entire; full: *a complete set of Mark Twain's writings.* Finished; ended; concluded. Having all the required or customary characteristics, skills, or the like; consummate; perfect in kind or quality: *a complete scholar.* Thorough; entire; total; undivided, uncompromised, or unmodified.

- **Com-ple-tion** *n.* The act of completing. The state of being completed. Conclusion; fulfillment: *Her last novel represented the completion of her literary achievement.* Termination, ending, closing.

- **Com-pre-hend** *v.t.* To understand the nature or meaning of; grasp with the mind; perceive: *He did not comprehend the significance of the ambassador's remark.* To take in or embrace; include; comprise. To grasp; to know.

- **Con-scious** *adj.* Aware of one's own existence, sensations, thoughts, surroundings. Awake. Fully, or painfully aware of, sensitive to, concerned with, or worried about a particular matter, action, feeling, or something. Having the mental faculties fully active. Known to oneself; felt. Aware of what one is doing, aware of oneself, self-conscious, deliberate, intentional, acutely aware of, or concerned about right, and inwardly sensible of wrong-doing. The part of the mind comprising psychic material of which the individual is aware. Directly perceptible to and under the control of one's self.

- **Con-sist-ent** *adj.* Agreeing or accordant; compatible; not self-contradictory: *His views and actions are consistent.* Constantly adhering to the same principles, course, form, etc.: *a consistent opponent.* Holding firmly together; cohering. Fixed; firm. **Con-sist-ent-ly,** *adv.*

- **Con-sult** *v.* To seek advice or information from; ask guidance from: *Consult your lawyer before signing the contract.* To refer to for information: *Consult your dictionary for the spelling of the word.* To have regard for (a person's interest, convenience, etc.) in making plans. To meditate, plan, or contrive. To consider or deliberate; take counsel; confer (usually followed by *with*): *He consulted with his doctor.* To give professional or expert advice; serve as consultant. A consultation.

- **Con-tam-i-nate** *v., n., adj.* To make impure or unsuitable by contact or mixture with something unclean, bad, etc.: *to contaminate a lake with sewage.* To render harmful or unusable by adding radioactive material to: *to contaminate a laboratory.* Something that contaminates or carries contamination; contaminant. Defile, pollute, taint, infect, poison, corrupt.

- **Con-tem-plate** *v.* To look at or view with continued attention; observe or study thoughtfully: *to contemplate the stars.* To consider thoroughly; think fully or deeply about: *to contemplate a difficult problem.* To have as a purpose; intend. To have in view as a future event: *to contemplate buying a new car.* To think studiously; meditate; consider deliberately. To survey, observe, gaze at, behold, regard, survey, study, ponder, design, plan. **Con-tem-plat-ing,** *adv.*

- **Con-vey** *v.t.* To carry, bring, or take from one place to another; transport; bear. To communicate; impart; make known: *to convey a wish.* To lead or conduct, as a channel or medium; transmit. To transfer; pass the title to. To move. See **carry.**

- **Cor-po-rate** *adj.* To make into a unified body endowed by *"LAW"* with the rights and liabilities of an individual. See corporation.

- **Cor-po-ra-tion** *n.* A group united—the municipal authorities. A body formed and authorized by *"LAW"* to act as a single person. An association of employers and employees as an organ of political representation. A paunch or potbelly! *AND* **from The D's Dictionary: Corporation** *n.* An ingenious device for obtaining individual profit **without individual responsibility**!

- **Cup** *n.,* A small, open container made of china, glass, metal, etc., usually having a handle and used chiefly as a receptacle from which to drink tea, soup, etc. Any cuplike utensil, organ, part, cavity, etc. To take or place in, or as in, a cup: *He cupped his ear with the palm of his hand.* To form into a cuplike shape: *He cupped his hands.* **Cupped**, *adj.*

- **Daz-zling** *v., n., v.t.* To overpower or dim the vision of by intense light: *He was dazzled by the sudden sunlight.* To impress deeply; astonish with delight: *The glorious palace dazzled him v.i.* To shine or reflect brilliantly: *gems dazzling in the sunlight.* To be overpowered by light: *Her eyes dazzled in the glare.* To excite admiration by brilliance: *Once one is accustomed to such splendor, it no longer dazzles.* An act or instance of dazzling: *the dazzle of the spotlights.* Something that dazzles. Awe, overwhelm, overpower, stupefy. *Daz-zles, n.*

- **De-ci-sive** *adj.* Having the power or quality of deciding; putting an end to controversy; crucial or most important: *Your argument was the decisive one.* Characterized by or displaying no or little hesitation; resolute; determined: *The general was known for his decisive manner.* Indisputable; definite: *a decisive defeat.* Unsurpassable; commanding; conclusive, final, firm.

- **De-fi-ance** *n.* A daring or bold resistance to authority or to any opposing force. Open disregard; contempt; often followed by *of*: *defiance of danger; his refusal amounted to defiance.* A challenge to meet in combat or in a contest. To offer resistance; defy. In defiance of; in spite of; notwithstanding.

- **De-lib-er-ate** *adj., v.* Carefully weighed or considered; studied; intentional: *a deliberate lie.* Characterized by deliberation; careful or slow in deciding. Leisurely and steady in movement or action; slow and even; unhurried: *a deliberate step.* To weigh in the mind; consider: *to deliberate a question.* To think carefully or attentively; reflect: *She deliberated for a long time before giving her decision.* To consult or confer formally: *The jury deliberated for three hours.* **De-lib-er-ate-ly,** *adv.*

- **De-pend-a-ble** *adj.* Capable of being depended on; worthy of trust; reliable: *a de-*

pendable employee. Trustworthy, responsible, trusty, trusted, steadfast, faithful.

- **Dip-lo-mat-ic** *adj.* Of, pertaining to, or engaged in diplomacy: *diplomatic officials.* Skilled in dealing with sensitive matters or people; tactful. **Dip-lo-mat-i-cal-ly,** *adv.*

- **Di-rec-tive** *adj.* Serving to direct; directing: *a directive board. Psychol.* pertaining to a type of psychotherapy in which the therapist actively offers advice and information rather than dealing only with information supplied by the patient. An authoritative instruction or direction; a specific order.

- **Drib-ble** *v.* To fall or flow in drops or small quantities; trickle; to drivel; slaver; to let fall in drops. A small trickling stream or a drop. A small quantity of anything. **Drib-bling,** *n.*

- **Ef-fer-vesce** *v.i.* To give off bubbles of gas, as fermenting liquors. To issue forth in bubbles. To show enthusiasm, excitement, liveliness, etc.: *The parents effervesced with pride over their new baby.* **Ef-fer-ves-cence,** *n.*

- **Em-a-nate** *v.* To flow out, issue, or proceed, as from a source or origin; come forth; originate. To send forth; emit. Arise, spring, flow. See **emerge. Em-i-nat-ing.** *v.i.*

- **En-cour-age** *v.t.* To inspire with courage,

spirit, or confidence: *His coach encouraged him throughout the marathon race to keep on running.* To stimulate by assistance, approval, etc.: *One of the chief duties of a teacher is to encourage students.* To promote, advance, or foster: *Poverty often encourages crime.* Embolden, hearten, reassure, urge; support, aid, help.

- **E-qua-nim-ity** *n.* Mental or emotional stability or composure, especially under tension or strain; calmness; equilibrium. Even, plain, equal + *anim(us)* mind, spirit, feelings; serenity, self-possession, aplomb.

- **Ex-cep-tion-al** *adj.* Forming an exception or rare instance; unusual; extraordinary: *The warm weather was exceptional for January.* Unusually excellent; superior: *an exceptional violinist.* Being intellectually gifted. Being physically or especially mentally handicapped to an extent that special schooling is required. Uncommon, singular, strange, unnatural, aberrant, anomalous.

- **Ex-ist-ence** *n.* The state or fact of existing; being. Continuance in being or life; life: *a struggle for existence.* Mode of existing: *They were working for a better existence.* All that exists: *Existence shows a universal order.* Something that exists; entity; being.

- **Ex-plic-it** *adj.* Fully and clearly expressed or

demonstrated; leaving nothing merely implied; unequivocal: *explicit instructions* Clearly developed or formulated: *explicit knowledge; explicit belief.* Definite and unreserved in expression; outspoken: *He was quite explicit as to what he expected us to do for him.* Described or shown in realistic detail. Express, definite, precise, exact, unambiguous. Open, forthright, unabashed. **Ex-plic-it-ly,** *adv.*

- **Fa-cil-i-tate** *v.t.* To make easier or less difficult; help forward (an action, a process, etc.): *Careful planning facilitates any kind of work.* To assist the progress of (a person). **Fa-cil-i-tat-ed,** *v.t.*

- **Fer-vent** *adj.* Having, showing, or displaying a passionate intensity; great warmth or intensity of spirit, feeling, enthusiasm, ardent; hot; burning; glowing. Also, fervid, impassioned, passionate.

- **Fla-grant** *adj.* Shockingly noticeable or evident; obvious; glaring: *a flagrant error.* Notorious; scandalous: *a flagrant crime; a flagrant offender.* Blazing, burning, or glowing; to burn; disgraceful, monstrous, egregious. FLAGRANT, GLARING, GROSS, OUTRAGEOUS, RANK are adjectives suggesting extreme offensiveness. FLAGRANT, with a root sense of flaming or flaring, suggests evil or immorality so evident that it cannot be ignored or overlooked: *a flagrant violation of the law.*

- **Flit** *v.* To move lightly and swiftly; fly, dart, or skim along: *bees flitting from flower to flower.* To flutter, as a bird. To pass quickly, as time: *hours flitting by.* A light, swift movement; flutter. See fly. **Flit-ted,** *n.*

- **Flut-ter** *v.i.* To wave, flap, or toss about: *Banners fluttered in the breeze.* To flap the wings rapidly; fly with flapping movements. To move in quick, irregular motions; vibrate. To beat rapidly, as the heart. To be tremulous or agitated. To go with irregular motions or aimless course: *to flutter back and forth.* To cause to flutter; vibrate; agitate. To throw into nervous or tremulous excitement; cause mental agitation; confuse. A fluttering movement: *He made little nervous flutters with his hands.* A state of nervous excitement or mental agitation: *a flutter of anticipation.* flurry, twitter, stir, dither. **Flut-ter-ed,** *n.*

- **Forth-right** *adj., n.* Going straight to the point; frank; direct; outspoken: *It's sometimes difficult to be forthright and not give offense.* Proceeding in a straight course; direct; straightforward: *a forthright glance.* Also, **Forth-right-ly** *adv., n.* Straight or directly forward; in a direct or straightforward manner: *He told us forthright just what his objections were.* Straightaway; at once; immediately: *He saw forthright that such an action* *was folly.* A straight course or path.

- **Frag-ment** *n.* A part broken off or detached: *scattered fragments of the broken vase.* An isolated, unfinished, or incomplete part: *She played a fragment of her latest composition.* An odd piece, bit, or scrap. To collapse or break into fragments; disintegrate: *The chair fragmented under his weight.* To break (something) into pieces or fragments; cause to disintegrate: *Outside influences soon fragmented the Mayan culture.* To divide into fragments; disunify. A broken piece, remnant.

- **Hor-ren-dous** *adj.* Shockingly dreadful; horrible: *a horrendous crime.* Dreadful, to be feared; to bristle, shudder; appalling, frightful, hideous.

- **Hump** *n.* A rounded protuberance, especially a fleshy protuberance on the back, as that due to abnormal curvature of the spine in humans, or that normally present in certain animals, as the camel or bison. A low, rounded rise of ground; hummock. A mountain or mountain range. **Over the hump,** past the most difficult, time-consuming, or dangerous part or period: *The doctor says she's over the hump now and should improve steadily.* To raise (the back) in a hump; hunch: *The cat humped its back.*

- **Ig-nore** *v.* To refrain from noticing or recognizing: *to ignore insulting remarks.* To reject, to not know, to disregard, as if unaware of existence!

- **Im-bal-ance** *n.* The state or condition of lacking balance, as in proportion or distribution. A faulty muscular or glandular coordination.

- **In-ap-pro-pri-ate** *adj.* Not proper, appropriate, or suitable; improper, unsuitable, inapt, unfitting. Improper in the circumstance; without permission; lacking devotion to the purpose at hand; crass, lacking sensitivity, refinement, or intelligence.

- **In-ci-dent** *n.* An individual occurrence or event. A distinct piece of action, or an episode, as in a story or play. Something that occurs casually in connection with, or appertaining to, or attaching to something else. An occurrence of seemingly minor importance; or, a violent event, such as a fracas or assault. A hostile clash between forces of rivals. A case or instance of something happening; the occurrence of dangerous, or exciting things. An embarrassing occurrence, especially of a social nature. Likely or apt to happen. Naturally appertaining.

- **In-cred-i-ble** *adj.* So extraordinary as to seem impossible: *incredible speed.* Not credible; hard to believe; unbelievable: *The plot of* *the book is incredible.* Farfetched, astonishing, preposterous. **In-cred-i-bly,** *adv.*

- **In-doc-tri-nate** *v.t.* To instruct in a doctrine, principle, ideology, etc., especially to imbue with a specific partisan or biased belief or point of view. To teach or inculcate. To imbue with learning; brainwash, propagandize.

- **In-tim-i-date** *v.t.* To frighten or overawe someone, especially in order to make them do what one wants. To make timid; fill with fear. To overawe or cow, as through the force of personality, or by superior display of wealth, talent, noise, loudness, etc. To force into, or deter from, some action by inducing fear! To make afraid!

- **In-te-grate** *v.* To bring together or incorporate (parts) into a whole. To make up, combine, or complete to produce a whole or a larger unit, as parts do. To unite or combine. *__To give or cause to give equal opportunity and consideration to (a racial, religious, or ethnic group or a member of such a group): to integrate minority groups in the school system. To combine (educational facilities, classes, and the like, previously segregated by race) into one unified system; to desegregate.__* __To give or cause to give members of all races, religions, and ethnic groups an equal opportunity to belong to, be employed by, be customers of, or vote in (an__

81

organization, place of business, city, state, etc.): to integrate a restaurant; to integrate a country club. *Mathematics:* to find the integral of. To indicate the total amount or the mean value of, meld with, become part of the dominant culture. To perform the operation of integration; find solution to a differential equation; renew, restore; merge, unify, fuse, mingle. **And from the author of this book: Wow-eee!! One great word!! Too bad that MANkind has been** *unable . . .* **NO,** *incapable* of having the necessary **ability, qualification**, and **strength** to perform this straightforward, specified act, and function. **Nor has MANkind even tried to live up to its real meaning! What pee brains!!!**

- **Ir-i-des-cent** *adj.* Displaying a play of lustrous colors like those of the rainbow. An iridescent cloth, material, or other substance.

- **Jus-tice** *n.* The quality of being just; righteousness, equitableness, or moral rightness: *to uphold the justice of a cause.* Rightfulness or lawfulness, as of a claim or title; justness of ground or reason: *to complain with justice.* The moral principle determining just conduct. Conformity to this principle, as manifested in conduct; just conduct, dealing, or treatment. The administering of deserved punishment or reward. The maintenance or administration of what is just by law, as by judicial or other proceedings: *a court of justice.* Judgment of persons or causes by judicial process: *to administer justice in a community.* A judicial officer; a judge or magistrate. Also called **Justice Department.** The Department of Justice. **Bring to justice,** to cause to come before a court for trial or to receive punishment for one's misdeeds: *The murderer was brought to justice.* **To do justice.** To act or treat justly or fairly. To appreciate properly: *We must see this play again to do it justice.* To acquit in accordance with one's abilities or potentialities. ___*AND* **from The D's Dictionary:**___ A commodity which in a more or less adulterated condition the State sells to the citizen as a reward for his allegiance, taxes, and {clear your throat for this} *personal service!*

- **Know** *v., n.* To perceive or understand as fact or truth; to apprehend clearly and with certainty. To have established or fixed in the mind or memory. To be absolutely certain or sure about something: *I know it.* To be acquainted with (a thing, place, person, etc.), as by sight, experience, or report. To understand from experience or attainment. To be able to distinguish, as one from another: *to know right from wrong.* To have knowledge, or clear and certain perception, as of fact, or truth. To be cognizant or aware of, as of some act, circumstance, or occurrence through observation, inquiry, or information; to have information, as about something. To understand or be familiar with the particulars of a subject, the facts, or state of knowing; knowledge. Possessing inside, secret, or special information.

- **Law** *n.* The principles and regulations established in a community by some authority and applicable to its people, whether in the form of legislation or of custom and policies recognized and enforced by judicial decision. Any written or positive rule or collection of rules prescribed under the authority of the state or nation, as by the people in its constitution. **Bylaw; Statute law.** The controlling influence of such rules; the condition of society brought about by their observance: *maintaining law and order.* A system or collection of such rules. The department of knowledge concerned with these rules; jurisprudence: *to study law.* The body of such rules concerned with a particular subject or derived from a particular source: *commercial law.* An act of the supreme legislative body of a state or nation, as distinguished from the constitution. The principles applied in the courts of common law, as distinguished from equity. The profession that deals with law and legal procedure: *to practice law.* Legal action; litigation. A person, group, or agency acting officially to enforce the law: *The law arrived at the scene soon after the alarm went off.* Any rule or injunction that must be obeyed: *Having a nourishing breakfast was an absolute* *law in our household.* A rule or principle of proper conduct sanctioned by conscience, concepts of natural justice, or the will of a deity: *a moral law.* A rule or manner of behavior that is instinctive or spontaneous: *the law of self-preservation.* In philosophy, science, etc.: **a.** a statement of a relation or sequence of phenomena invariable under the same conditions. **b.** a mathematical rule. A principle based on the predictable consequences of an act, condition, etc : *the law of supply and demand.* A rule, principle, or convention regarded as governing the structure or the relationship of an element in the structure of something, as of a language or work of art: *the laws of playwriting; the laws of grammar.* A commandment or a revelation from God. A divinely appointed order or system. **The Law.** See **Law of Moses.** The preceptive part of the Bible, especially of the New Testament, in contradistinction to its promises: *the law of Christ.* Be a law to or unto oneself, to follow one's own inclinations, rules of behavior, etc.; act independently or unconventionally, especially without regard for established mores. **Lay down the law: a.** to state one's views authoritatively. **b.** to give a command in an imperious manner: *The manager laid down the law to the workers.* **Take the law into one's own hands,** to administer justice as one sees fit without recourse to the usual law enforcement or legal processes: *The townspeople took the law into* *their own hands before the sheriff took ac-tion.* __*AND*__ **from** **The D's Dictionary:** That which is compatible with the will of a judge having jurisdiction! **Law-ful** *adj.*

- **Law-yer** *n.* A person whose profession is to represent clients in a court of law or to advise or act for clients in other legal matters. *New Testament*: an interpreter of the Mosaic Law. Luke 14:3. *v.i.* To work as a lawyer; practice law. *v.t.* To submit (a case, document, or the like) to a lawyer for examination, advice, clarification, etc. **Lawyer-like, law-yer-ly,** *adj.* __*AND*__ **from** **The D's Dictionary:** One skilled in circumvention of the Law—especially for corporations, politicians, and others of wealth!

- **Leech** *n.* Any bloodsucking or carnivorous aquatic or terrestrial worm of the class Hirudinea, certain freshwater species of which were formerly much used in medicine for bloodletting. A person who clings to or hangs onto another for personal gain, especially without giving anything in return, and usually with the implication or effect of exhausting the other's resources; parasite. An instrument used for drawing blood. To apply leeches to, so as to bleed. To cling to and feed upon or drain, as a leech: *His relatives leeched him until his entire fortune was exhausted. Archaic.* to cure; heal. Bloodsucker; extortioner; sponger.

- **Light-ning** *n.* A brilliant electric spark discharge in the atmosphere, occurring within a thundercloud, between clouds, or between a cloud and the ground. To emit a flash or flashes of lightning (often used impersonally with *it* as subject): *If it starts to lightning, we'd better go inside.* Of, pertaining to, or resembling lightning, especially in regard to speed of movement: *lightning flashes; lightning speed.*

- **Main-tained** *v.t.* To keep in existence or continuance; preserve; retain: *to maintain good relations with neighboring countries.* To keep in an appropriate condition, operation, or force; keep unimpaired: *to maintain order; to maintain public highways.* To keep in a specified state, position, etc.: *to maintain a correct posture; to maintain good health..* To affirm; assert; declare: *He maintained that the country was going downhill.* To support in speech or argument, as a statement or proposition. To keep or hold against attack: *to maintain one's ground.* To provide for the upkeep or support of; carry the expenses of: *to maintain a family.* To sustain or support: *not enough water to maintain life.* To continue, keep up, asseverate. MAINTAIN, ASSERT, AVER, ALLEGE, HOLD, STATE all mean to express an opinion, judgment, or position. MAINTAIN carries the implications of both firmness and persistence in declaring or supporting a conviction!

- **Man-i-fest** *adj*. Readily perceived by the eye or the understanding; evident; obvious; apparent; plain: *a manifest error. Psychoanal.* Of or pertaining to conscious feelings, ideas, and impulses that contain repressed psychic material: *the manifest content of a dream as opposed to the latent content that it conceals.* To make clear or evident to the eye or the understanding; show plainly: *He manifested his approval with a hearty laugh..* To prove; put beyond doubt or question: *The evidence manifests the guilt of the defendant.* To record in a ship's manifest; a list of the cargo carried by a ship, made for the use of various agents and officials at the ports of destination. A list or invoice of goods transported by truck or train; a list of the cargo or passengers carried on an airplane. Detected in the act, evident, visible, clear, distinct, unmistakable, patent, open, palpable, visible, conspicuous. To reveal, disclose, evince, evidence, demonstrate, declare, express.

- **Meta-morph-ic** *adj*. Pertaining to or characterized by change of form, or metamorphosis.

- **Met-a-mor-phose** *v.*, to change the form or nature of; transform. To subject to metamorphosis or metamorphism. To undergo or be capable of undergoing a change in form or nature. Mutate, transmute.

- **Met-a-mor-pho-sis** *n.*, A profound change in

form from one stage to the next in the life history of an organism, as from the caterpillar to the pupa and from the pupa to the adult butterfly. **Complete metamorphosis.** A complete change of form, structure, or substance, as if transformation by magic or witchcraft. Any complete change in appearance, character, circumstances, etc.; a form resulting from any such change. Transformation. Mutation. Transmutation.

- **Mi'-nute'** *adj.* Extremely small, as in size, amount, extent, or degree. So small as to verge on insignificance. Or, taking the smallest points into consideration; attentive to or concerned with even the smallest details. To make smaller or fewer; tiny, infinitesimal, minuscule, little, detailed, exact; precise and meticulous.

- **Ob-tect** *adj.* (of a pupa) having the antennae, legs, and wings glued to the surface of the body.

- **Of-fen-sive** *adj.* Causing resentful displeasure; highly irritating, angering, or annoying: *offensive television commercials.* Unpleasant or disagreeable to the sense: *an offensive odor.* Repugnant to the moral sense, good taste, or the like; insulting: *an offensive remark; an offensive joke.* Pertaining to offense or attack: *the offensive movements of their troops.* Characterized by attack; aggressive:

offensive warfare. The position or attitude of aggression, aggressive movement, or attack: *to take the offensive* Displeasing, vexatious, vexing, unpleasant. See hateful. Distasteful, disgusting, revolting.

- **Par-ti-cles** *n.* A minute or mi'nute' portion, piece, fragment, or amount; a tiny or very small bit: *a particle of dust; not a particle of supporting evidence.* One of the extremely small constituents of matter, as an atom or nucleus. An elementary particle, quark, or gluon. A body in which the internal motion is negligible. In some languages one of the major form classes of speech, consisting of words that are neither nouns nor verbs, or of all uninflected words, or the like. A small word of functional or relational use, as an article, preposition, or conjunction, whether of a separate form class or not. A small piece, mite, whit, iota, jot, tittle, grain, speck.

- **Perf-ect** *adj.* Conforming absolutely to the description or definition of an ideal type: *a perfect sphere; a perfect gentleman.* Excellent or complete beyond practical or theoretical improvement: *There is no perfect legal code. The proportions of this temple are almost perfect.* Exactly fitting the need in a certain situation or for a certain purpose: *a perfect actor to play Mr. Micawber; a perfect saw for cutting out keyholes.* Entirely without any flaws, defects, or shortcomings: *a perfect* *apple; the perfect crime.* Accurate, exact, or correct in every detail: *a perfect copy.* Thorough; complete; utter: *perfect strangers.* Pure or unmixed: *perfect yellow.* Unqualified; absolute: *He has perfect control over his followers.* Expert; accomplished; proficient. Unmitigated; out-and-out; of an extreme degree: *He made a perfect fool of himself.* Complete. Unblemished; faultless.

* **Phan-tas-ma-go-ri-a** *n.* A shifting series of phantasms, illusions, or deceptive appearances, as in a dream or as created by the imagination. A changing scene made up of many elements. An optical illusion produced by a magic lantern or the like in which figures increase or diminish in size, pass into each other, dissolve, etc.

* **Pol-i-ti-cian** *n.* A person who is active in party politics. A seeker or holder of public office, who is more concerned about winning favor or retaining power than about maintaining principles. A person who holds a political office. A person skilled in political government or administration; statesman or stateswoman. An expert in politics or political government. A person who seeks to gain power or advancement within an organization in ways that are generally disapproved. POLITICIAN, STATESMAN refer to one skilled in politics. These terms differ particularly in their connotations; POLITICIAN is more often de-

rogatory, and STATESMAN laudatory. POLITI-CIAN suggests the schemes and devices of a person who engages in (especially small) politics for party ends or for one's own advantage: *a dishonest politician.* **_AND_ from the D's Dictionary:** *n.* An eel in the fundamental mud upon which the superstructure of organized society is reared. When he wriggles he mistakes the agitation of his tail for the trembling of the edifice. As compared with the statesman, he suffers the disadvantage of being alive!

- **Pol-i-tics** *n. (used with a singular or plural. v.)* The science or art of political government. The practice or profession of conducting political affairs. Political methods or maneuvers. Political principles or opinions. Use of intrigue or strategy in obtaining any position of power or control, as in business, university, etc. To engage in political intrigue, take advantage of a political situation or issue, resort to partisan politics, etc.; exploit a political system or political relationships. To deal with people in an opportunistic, manipulative, or devious way, as for job advancement. **_AND_ from The D's Dictionary:** *n.* A strife of interests masquerading as a contest of principles. The conduct of public affairs for private advantage!

- **Poop,** *Slang. n.* Excrement. Feces. To defecate. **Pooped,** *adj.* Also, pee brain, poophead.

- **Prat-tle** *v.* To talk in a foolish or simple-minded way; chatter; babble. To utter by chattering or babbling. The act of prattling. Gab, jabber, gabble, blab.

- **Pul-sate** *n.* The act of pulsating; beating or throbbing. A beat or throb, as of the pulse. Vibration or undulation. A single vibration.

- **Quell** *v.t.* To suppress; put an end to; extinguish, vanquish, subdue. To quiet or allay (emotions, anxieties, etc.): *The child's mother quelled his fears of the thunder.* Crush, quash, overpower, overcome, defeat, conquer, quench, calm, pacify, compose, hush.

- **Re-spons-i-ble** *adj.* Answerable or accountable, as for something within one's power, control, or management (often followed by *to* or *for*): *He is responsible to the president for his decisions.* Involving accountability or responsibility: *a responsible position.* Chargeable with being the author, cause, or occasion of something (usually followed by *for*): *Termites were responsible for the damage.* Having a capacity for moral decisions and therefore accountable; capable of rational thought or action: *The defendant is not responsible for his actions.* Able to discharge obligations or pay debts. Reliable or dependable, as in meeting debts, conducting business dealings, etc. (Of a government, member of a government, government agency, or the like—

answerable to or serving at the discretion of an elected legislature or the electorate.) Liable. Competent. Solvent. Honest, capable, reliable, trustworthy.

- **Scamp-er** *v.i.* To run or go hastily or quickly. To run playfully about, as a child. A scampering; a quick run. **Scamp-ered** *n.*

- **Sear-ing** *v.t.* To burn or char the surface of: *She seared the steak to seal in the juices.* To mark with a branding iron. To burn or scorch injuriously or painfully: *He seared his hand on a hot steam pipe.* To make callous or unfeeling; harden: *The hardship of her youth has seared her emotionally.* To dry up or wither; parch. To become dry or withered, as vegetation. A mark or scar made by searing.

- **Si-mul-ta-ne-ous** *adj.* Existing, occurring, operating, or done at the same time; concurrent; simultaneous movements; simultaneous translation. Together, similar, instantaneous, synchronous, coincident, exact, accurate, careful; absolute precision; mechanical or scientific exactness.

- **Spec-tac-u-lar** *adj.* Of or like a spectacle; marked by or given to an impressive, large-scale display. Dramatically daring or thrilling: *a spectacular dive from a cliff.* A single television production featuring well-known performers and characterized by elaborate

94

sets, costumes, staging, etc. An impressive, large-scale display: *another Hollywood spectacular.* Hair-raising, dramatic, breathtaking.

- **Spir-it** *n.* The principle of conscious life; the vital principle in humans, animating the body or mediating between body and soul. The incorporeal part of humans: *present in spirit though absent in body.* The soul regarded as separating from the body at death. Conscious, incorporeal being, as opposed to matter. **The Spirit, God.** Life, mind, consciousness, essence. An attitude or principle that inspires, animates, or pervades thought, feeling, or action: *the spirit of reform.* The divine influence as an agency working in the human heart. A divine, inspiring, or animating being or influence. Num. 11:25; Is. 32:15. The third person of the Trinity; Holy Spirit. The soul or heart as the seat of feelings or sentiments, or as prompting to action: *a man of broken spirit.* Spirits, feelings or mood with regard to exaltation or depression: *low spirits; good spirits.* Excellent disposition or attitude in terms of vigor, courage, firmness of intent, etc.; mettle: *That's the spirit!* Temper or disposition: *meek in spirit.* An individual as characterized by a given attitude, disposition, character, action, etc.: *A few brave spirits remained to face the danger.* The dominant tendency or character of anything: *the spirit of the age.* Vigorous sense of membership in a group: *college spirit.* The general meaning or intent of a statement, document, etc.: *the spirit of the law.* Out of spirits, in low spirits; depressed: *We were feeling out of spirits after so many days of rain.* Life, mind, consciousness, essence, genius, enthusiasm, energy, zeal, and/or, fire, enterprise. Attitude, mood, humor, nature, drift, tenor, gist, essence, sense.

- **Straight-for-ward** *adj.* Going or directed straight ahead: *a straightforward gaze.* Direct; not roundabout: *a straightforward approach to a problem.* Free from crookedness or deceit; honest: *straightforward in one's dealings.* Also, **straight-for-wards** straight ahead; directly or continuously forward. Undeviating, unswerving.

- **Swag-ger** *v.i.* To walk or strut with a defiant or insolent air. To boast or brag noisily. To bring, drive, force, etc., by blustering. In a swaggering manner, conduct, or walk; ostentatious display of arrogance and conceit. See **strut. Swag-ger-ing** *adj.* Pertaining to, characteristic of, or behaving in the manner of a person who swaggers.

- **Sym-bol** *n., v.* Something used for or regarded as representing or standing for something else; a material object representing something abstract—or visa versa, often something immaterial; emblem, token, or sign. A letter, shape, figure, sign, other character, or mark, or a combination of letters, or the like used to designate something. A word, phrase, image, or the like having a complex of associated meanings and perceived as having inherent value separable from or part of that which is symbolized and as performing its normal function of standing for, or representing, that which is symbolized; usually conceived as deriving its meaning chiefly from the structure in which it appears, and generally distinguished from a sign

- **Syn-chro-nous** *adj.* Occurring at the same time; coinciding in time; contemporaneous; simultaneous; going on at the same rate and exactly together; recurring together.

- **Trans-lu-cent** *adj.* Permitting light to pass through but diffusing it so that persons, objects, etc., on the opposite side are not clearly visible: *Frosted window glass is translucent but not transparent.* Easily understandable; lucid. Clear. To shine through.

- **Un-flinch-ing** *adj.* Not flinching; unshrinking: *unflinching courage.* Steady, constant, steadfast, unfaltering.

- **U-nique** *adj.* Existing as the only one or as the sole example; single; solitary in type or characteristics. Having no like or equal; unparalleled; incomparable. Limited in occurrence to a given class, situation, or area: *a* *species unique to Australia.* Limited to a single outcome or result; without alternative possibilities. Not typical; unusual: *She has a very unique smile n.* The embodiment of unique characteristics; the only specimen of a given kind: *The unique is also the improbable.*

- **Un-speak-a-ble** *adj.* Not speakable; that may not be spoken. Exceeding the power of speech; unutterable; inexpressible; indescribable. Inexpressibly bad or objectionable. Ineffable, unimaginable.

- **Vi-va-cious** *adj.* Lively; animated; gay: *a vivacious folk dance.* Spirited, brisk.

- **Viv-id** *adj.* Strikingly bright or intense, as color, light, etc.: *a vivid green.* Full of life; lively; animated: *a vivid personality.* Presenting the appearance, freshness, spirit, etc., of life; realistic: *a vivid account.* Strong, distinct, or clearly perceptible: *a vivid recollection.* Forming distinct and striking mental images: *a vivid imagination.* Bright, brilliant, intense. Spirited, vivacious. See picturesque.

- **Waft** *v.t.* To carry lightly and smoothly through the air or over water. To send or convey lightly, as if in flight. To signal to, summon, or direct by waving. To float or be carried, especially through the air. A sound, odor, etc., faintly perceived: *a waft of per-*

fume. A wafting movement; light current or gust: *a waft of air.* The act of wafting.

- **Warp** *v.t.* To bend or twist out of shape, especially from a straight or flat form, as timbers or flooring. To bend or turn from the natural or true direction or course. To distort or cause to distort from the truth, fact, true meaning, etc.; bias; falsify: *Prejudice warps the mind.* To become bent or twisted out of shape, especially out of a straight or flat form: *The wood has warped in drying.* To be or become biased; hold or change an opinion due to prejudice, external influence, or the like. A mental twist, bias, or quirk, or a biased or twisted attitude or judgment. A situation, environment, etc., that seems characteristic of another era, especially in being out of touch with contemporary life or attitudes, etc.; turn, contort, distort, swerve, deviate.

- **Whoa** *interj.* Stop! (used especially with or to horses).

- **Won-der** *v.i.* To think or speculate curiously: *to wonder about the origin of the solar system.* To be filled with admiration, amazement, or awe; marvel. To doubt. To speculate curiously or be curious about; be curious to know: *to wonder what happened.* To feel wonder at. Something strange and surprising; a cause of surprise, astonishment, or admiration. The emotion excited by what is strange and surprising; a feeling of surprised or puzzled interest, sometimes tinged with admiration. Miraculous deed or event; remarkable phenomenon. **For a wonder,** as the reverse of what might be expected; surprisingly: *For a wonder, they worked hard all day.* Conjecture, meditate, ponder, question.

- **Yap** *v.* To bark sharply, shrilly, or snappishly; yelp. *Slang.* to talk shrilly, noisily, or foolishly. To utter by yapping. A sharp, shrill, or snappish bark; yelp. *Slang.* Shrill, noisy, or foolish talk. The mouth: *Keep your yap shut. Slang.* An uncouth or stupid person; bumpkin; fool.

References:

—Bible
—*Random House Webster's Dictionary*
—*Merriam-Webster's Collegiate Dictionary*
—*Oxford English Dictionary*
—*Metaphysical Dictionary*
—*Grapho Analysis Dictionary*
—*The New Dictionary of Thoughts*
—*The Devil's Dictionary*

Combined Dictionary Definitions are from:

—Random House Webster's Dictionary
—Merriam-Webster's Collegiate Dictionary
—Oxford English Dictionary

The relation is very close
between our capacity to act at all
and our conviction
that the action we are taking
is right.

. . . Without that belief,
most men will not have the energy
and the will
to persevere in the action!

Walter Lippman

*"It is a psychological truism
that the value and meaning
attached to an object
or to an idea
is in direct relation
to the inner need.*

*This inner need
finds expression
through
symbol formation."*

Unknown

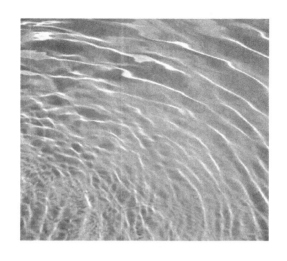

*"As soon as
the mental atmosphere
ceases to be able to affect us,
we are beginning to affect it.*

*The stabilized
inner atmosphere
overflows, and*

*The circle of harmony
spreads
like the ripples in a pool."*

Unknown

Butterflies,
like people,
range in appearance
and demeanor
from plain to

Even Spectacular!

But every now and again
along comes one
that is unusual,
different,
remarkable.

Even Unique!

*"At that point in life where your talents
meet the needs of the world, that is where
Spirit wants you to be!"*

Unknown

About The Author

Lois B. Barnes, 79, has worked for various publications and newspapers over the years, receiving on the job training. Additionally, she set the 18-point size type for the Missouri State Publication for the legally blind, prepared and published several small newsletters among which were *Wakela Speaks* for Cub Scouts when her  son was a member, *Life Lines* for the Missouri Press Women Association, *The Graphoanalyst* for the Kansas City, Mo., chapter of the International Graphoanalysis Society, Inc., *Community Newsletter* for Country Villa Estates Home Owners Association—her time and work freely given! She has had several articles published in the Pleasant Hill Times and the Blue Springs Sentinel. She wrote a Journalism Publication Manual for High School students, winning First place in the Missouri contest and Third in the National Competition held in Scottsdale, AZ. She lives and works from her home in a Retirement Community in Florida. BUTTERFLY! is her first book. She is currently working on her next release.